SNACK TIME, TYRANNOSAURUS REX!

based on text by Dawn Bentley

Illustrated by Karen Carr

Little®
Soundprints

For Tyler William. Love, Aunt Dawn. — D.B.

Dedicated with love to my husband, Ralph, and daughter, Jo. — K.C.

Published by Soundprints Division of Trudy Corporation, Norwalk, Connecticut.

Book design: Marcin Pilchowski
Editor: Laura Gates Galvin
Editorial assistance: Brian E. Giblin

First Edition 2004
10 9 8 7 6 5 4 3 2 1
Printed in China

Acknowledgements:
Our very special thanks to Dr. Brett-Surman of the Smithsonian Institution's National Museum of Natural History.
Soundprints would also like to thank Ellen Nanney and Katie Mann of the Smithsonian Institution for their help in the creation of this book.

Library of Congress Cataloging-in-Publication Data is
on file with the publisher and the Library of Congress.

SNACK TIME,
TYRANNOSAURUS REX!

based on text by Dawn Bentley

Illustrated by Karen Carr

A note to the reader:
Throughout this story you will see words in **bold letters**. There is more information about these words in the glossary. The glossary is in the back of the book.

Birds chirp. Insects buzz. Animals splash in a stream. Then a loud pounding sound fills the air. It's a Tyrannosaurus rex!

Tyrannosaurus rex
is very hungry.
She hopes to
find something
good to eat.

A **Quetzalcoatlus** flies by. Tyrannosaurus rex snaps at the reptile, but she misses. The Quetzalcoatlus flies away.

Tyrannosaurus rex
smells lunch!
Something moves
in the stream.
Tyrannosaurus rex
goes to the stream.

She walks into the water. She almost steps on a crocodile hiding in the **reeds**!

Now Tyrannosaurus rex sees what smelled good! It's a **Triceratops**. She chases him.

The Triceratops is ready to fight. He points his horns at Tyrannosaurus rex. She decides to look for another meal!

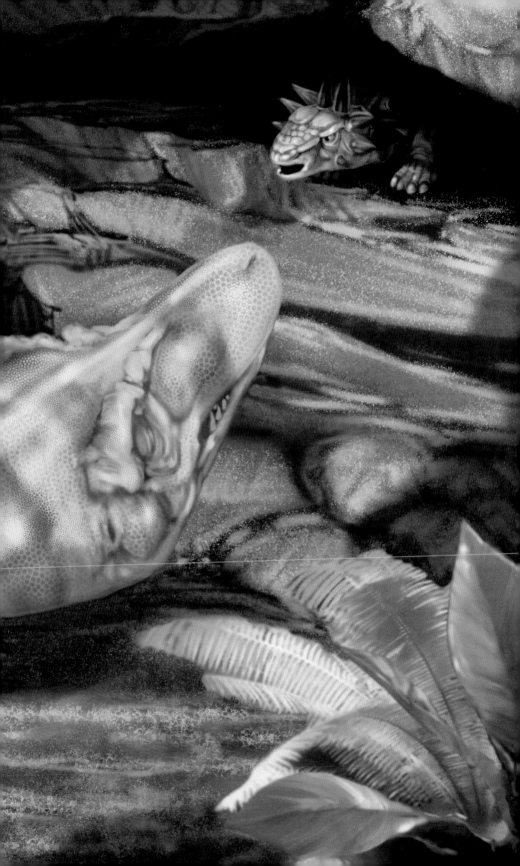

Tyrannosaurus rex sees an **Ankylosaurus** hiding in the rocks. She tries to reach him. She snaps at the young dinosaur, but she misses.

Tyrannosaurus rex snaps at the baby again. This time she bites into a rock. Crack! She breaks one of her teeth!

Tyrannosaurus rex
chases a small
Anatotitan. It took
all day to find lunch,
and now she can
finally eat it.

A volcano is erupting!
Tyrannosaurus rex is
powerful. But a volcano
is even more powerful!
Tyrannosaurus rex runs
to where she can once
again be the most
powerful thing of all!

Glossary

Anatotitan: One of the last dinosaurs. Its most distinguishing and unusual feature was its duckbill.

Ankylosaurus: *Ankylosaurus* had tough skin that was covered with bony plates, and it could swing its clubbed tail to protect itself from predators.

Quetzalcoatlus: A type of flying reptile which developed along with birds.

Reed: A tall, slender grass plant.

Triceratops: The biggest and heaviest of the horned dinosaurs. It weighed 11 tons and was nearly 30 feet long!

ABOUT *TYRANNOSAURUS REX*
(tye-RAN-oh-saur-us rex)

Tyrannosaurus rex roamed the earth 65 million years ago. *Tyrannosaurus rex* was the biggest meat-eating dinosaur on land at that time.

Tyrannosaurus rex was taller than a school bus! It weighed up to eight tons—that is more than two large elephants!

Tyrannosaurus rex had an excellent sense of smell and eyesight. *Tyrannosaurus rex* was faster than most plant-eating dinosaurs. These qualities made *Tyrannosaurus rex* a great hunter.

Other dinosaurs that lived with Tyrannosaurus rex:

Anatotitan (a-NAT-o-TIE-tan)

Ankylosaurus (ANG-ki-lo-SAWR-us)

Quetzalcoatlus (KWET-sal-coh-AT-lus)

Triceratops (try-SAIR-uh-tops)